W9-BNO-198

BUILDING AMERICA

New Netherland: The Dutch Settle the Hudson Valley

Mitchell Lane
PUBLISHERS

P.O. Box 196 • Hockessin, Delaware 19707

Titles in the Series

New Netherland: The Dutch Settle the Hudson Valley

Karen Bush Gibson

Printing   1   2   3   4   5   6   7   8   9

Library of Congress Cataloging-in-Publication Data
Gibson, Karen Bush.
    New Netherland: the Dutch Settle the Hudson Valley / by Karen Bush Gibson.
        p. cm.—(Building America)
    Includes bibliographical references and index.
    ISBN 1-58415-461-6 (library bound)
    1. Dutch—America—History—Juvenile literature. 2. Netherlands—Colonies—
America—History—Juvenile literature. 3. New Netherland—History—Juvenile
literature. 4. Netherlands—Commerce—America—History—Juvenile literature.
5. America—Commerce—Netherlands—History—Juvenile literature. I. Title.
II. Building America (Hockessin, Del.)
E184.D9G53 2006
974.7'302—dc22

                                             2005027978

ISBN-10:1-58415-461-6   ISBN-13: 978-1-58415-461-7

ABOUT THE AUTHOR: Karen Bush Gibson has written extensively for the juvenile educational market. Her work has included biographies, current events, and cultural histories, such as *The Life and Times of Catherine the Great*, *The Fury of Hurricane Andrew*, and *The Life and Times of John Peter Zenger* for Mitchell Lane Publishers. As one of a very few European republics during colonial settlement, the Netherlands had a strong impact on the formation of the United States. Karen believes that it's because of the Dutch influence that Americans have the liberties and freedoms they enjoy today.

PHOTO CREDITS: Cover, pp. 1, 3, 8, 17, 20, 30, 33, 38—North Wind Picture Archives; pp. 6, 12, 25, 41—Sharon Beck; p. 10—Old Galleries; pp. 14, 28, 34—Library of Congress; p. 36—Hulton Archive/Getty Images.

PUBLISHER'S NOTE: This story is based on the author's extensive research, which she believes to be accurate. Documentation of such research is contained on page 46.

    The internet sites referenced herein were active as of the publication date. Due to the fleeting nature of some web sites, we cannot guarantee they will all be active when you are reading this book.

Contents

*For Your Information

The Netherlands is a country of several provinces that joined together in the 1500s. Because it was a country of religious tolerance, people from other countries who were persecuted for their religious beliefs came to the Netherlands. This country prized education, science, and law and order. The Dutch were also important explorers, along with Britain, Spain, and France.

Chapter

1

Voyage to a New Land

The ocean slapped the sides of the ship as it moved through the blue-gray waters of the Atlantic Ocean. Taking care to avoid notice by the Spanish and the Portuguese, the Dutch ship sailed in a northwest-erly direction before arcing to the southwest. Pierre Monfort had seen nothing but water surrounding their ship, *Eendracht* (*Unity*), since leaving the Netherlands three months ago.

One of the first things Pierre learned to do was walk across the ship. It was harder than it looked as the ship rocked back and forth. But after a while, he found his sea legs, as one of the sailors called it. Unfortunately, the rocking had made his mother seasick. She stayed in bed most of the time.

Pierre and his family were part of the twenty-two families and fourteen single men on the first ship of settlers headed for the colony of New Netherland on the other side of the Atlantic Ocean. New Netherland was a land of forests and rivers. No towns or cities had been built there yet. It was a new land, a new world.

"And real Indians," he whispered to himself. He couldn't wait to see the Indian people he had heard so much about.

The families on board were to be the first permanent settlers from the Netherlands, a country sometimes called Holland. Holland is actually one of many provinces of the Netherlands. Most of the families were Walloons. Walloons were French-speaking people who had left their Belgian homes to the south for the religious freedom in the Netherlands.

The first settlers from the Netherlands were Walloons. These French-speaking people had gone to the Netherlands from Belgium, where they had been persecuted by the Spanish for their religious beliefs. Many of the refugees welcomed a chance to own property, build homes, and earn a living in a new land.

"Are you watching for land, lad?" Captain Adriaen Jorise said.

"Yes, sir, but I haven't seen any yet," Pierre answered.

"Keep looking, we should see land before the sun sets for the day."

Pierre looked until his eyes burned and only the black of night surrounded the ship, but he never saw land.

The next morning, Pierre sprang out of his bunk and onto the deck. It was a beautiful spring morning, with seagulls flying high in the clear blue sky. The air was still chilly, but noticeably warmer than it had been in the northern Atlantic. The bright sun warmed the deck of the ship.

Pierre had no trouble seeing the land today. It stretched in front of him. He looked left, and he looked right. Tinted green with spring, the land seemed to welcome them. Pierre looked around and saw all the men, women, and children on deck with smiles on their faces.

The ship dropped anchor at the Hartford River, where two families and six men left the ship. They took some supplies with them, including seeds and livestock. The *Unity* left two more families with eight men at the Delaware River. The ship rounded the southern end of an island called Manhattan. Eight men disembarked on a rounded part of the land jutting into the ocean. Pierre's father told him a trading post would be built nearby. While Manhattan lay on one side of the ship, a small island lay on the other. Pierre heard the men call it *Noten Eylandt*, or Nut Island, because of the walnut and chestnut trees there. There was talk of building a fort there. (Today, the island is known as Governors Island and is a protected historical area.)

Eighteen families remained on board the *Unity* as it headed north onto a wide river, which had tides like the ocean. Pierre knew Joris and Catelina Rapalje the best. Just nineteen and eighteen years of age, they had married four days before the *Unity* departed from Amsterdam on January 25, 1624.

The Dutch West India Company had told each of the families where they would establish a settlement. After ten years of service to the West India Company, the people would own their land. The families still on board would be settling about 150 miles up the river at Fort Orange, the first settlement in New Netherland and named after William (or Willem) the Silent of Orange in the Netherlands. Captain Jorise had told Pierre that this was a favorite trading place of the Indians.

By afternoon, Pierre couldn't wait to see his new home. As they traveled over the muddy water, rocky cliffs soared up high on the west side of the river. Pierre was speechless. He had never seen scenery like this in the flat land of the Netherlands.

Pierre soon heard a roaring sound. They must have been moving toward it, because it grew louder. Soon he saw that an impressive waterfall was making the noise. It sprayed the *Unity* before the ship turned from it and passed an island with an abandoned building. "That must

The Unity was one of the first ships to bring settlers from the Netherlands. Twenty-two families and approximately fourteen single men arrived with farming supplies.

be Fort Nassau," someone said. "Heard they had to leave it because of flooding."

Ahead of them lay a grove of huge pine trees. The crew dropped anchor, and everyone soon became busy loading items to row ashore. Pierre saw plenty of fish in the river. After he helped unload the supplies for the remaining settlers, Pierre took a long look around. Other people decided to look around and returned with juicy wild grapes. Pierre watched as his father nodded his approval at the rich black earth in his hands. Standing on land for the first time in a long while, they were now home.[1]

One of the earliest colonies in American history was the Dutch colony of *Nieuw Nederlandt*, or New Netherland, founded in 1621, only a year after the Pilgrims landed at Plymouth. Sometimes referred to as the middle colonies, this province included New York and parts of New Jersey, Connecticut, and Delaware. The creation and colonization of New Netherland by the Dutch is a significant episode in the colonial history of America.

Before the British claimed New York and New Jersey in 1664, the Netherlands had been colonizing the area for over forty years. New Netherland became a true melting pot, as the Dutch welcomed people from different countries to settle in the New World.

Seventeenth-Century Dutch Ships

During the seventeenth century, the Dutch were known for their fine ships. Many of the ships were similar in design and purpose, although no two were exactly alike. Shipbuilders didn't use blueprints or other written plans, but created ships from the ideas in their head.

In the late sixteenth and early seventeenth centuries, the Dutch East India Company sailed toward Asia in search of riches. They found success there with the spice trade. At its peak, the Dutch East India Company had 150 trading ships and 40 warships. One of the Dutch ships was the *Duyfken* (*Dove*), which became the first European ship to arrive in Australia. Ships sailing to America were similar to the *Duyfken*.

Duyfken

In the late 1990s, historians re-created the *Duyfken* for a reverse voyage, from Australia to the Netherlands. The *Duyfken* was a tall Dutch "jacht." The Dutch used many of these small jachts in their travels. (We now use the word *yacht* to describe pleasure boats.)

The hull of the *Duyfken* was built of oak from the northern European country of Latvia. Unlike other European shipbuilders, Dutch shipbuilders used a "plank-first" construction. After heating the planks with fire, the shipbuilders were able to bend them. The plank shell was held together by temporary cleats until full-sized timbers could be attached to the planks.

The *Duyfken* was not a large ship, but her (ships were always referred to as female) stern structure was high. The timbers of the back of the ship reached skyward. Four gun ports pierced the rail on each side. Once the deck beams were in place and secured to the hull, sails made from natural flax and hemp were fastened. There was usually a high deck called a poop deck on the back of the ship, with the captain's cabin underneath.

The Dutch ships of the seventeenth century were amazing in their ability to travel great distances powered solely by the wind on their sails. Because of the tall, sleek design, Dutch ships often out-sailed the bigger ships from other countries. The Dutch ships were stable with better-than-average maneuverability, which allowed them to go places bigger ships couldn't reach.

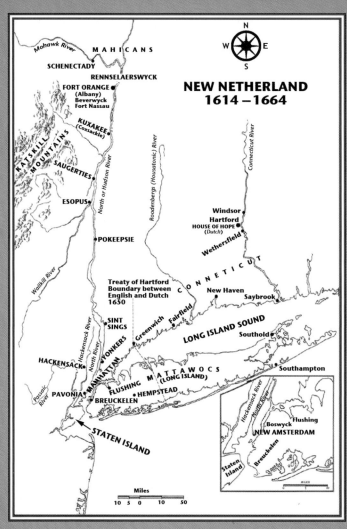

**NEW NETHERLAND
1614–1664**

New Netherland included New York and parts of New Jersey, Connecticut, and Delaware. It was discovered accidentally in 1609 when the Dutch government hired British explorer Henry Hudson to find a westward passage to Asia. He became the first European to explore what came to be called the Hudson River north of New York Harbor.

Chapter

2

New Netherland Discovered

Europeans had been sailing on the ocean searching for new lands for over a hundred years. The riches of Asia in the East, particularly in China, spurred Spain, England, France, and the Netherlands to look for new routes and new lands.

Like Christopher Columbus, a fellow Genoese named John Cabot explored uncharted territories for another country. Cabot, working for Britain, explored the coast of eastern North America from Newfoundland, Canada, to Delaware. Meanwhile, Spain was also making significant progress exploring the New World. They had established St. Augustine (Florida), the first permanent settlement by Europeans, in 1565.

Many countries in northern Europe were under the control of Spain in the early 1500s. Spain insisted on forcing the Roman Catholic religion on the heavily Protestant countries, and on punishing the Protestants. By 1566, people in these northern countries began rebelling. Willem the Silent of Orange was the leader in the Dutch quest for independence. In 1579, several provinces—Holland, Zeeland, Gelderland, Frisia (Friesland), Groningen, Utrecht, Overijssel—joined

Around 1450, Giovanni Caboto was born in Genoa, Italy, as the son of a spice merchant. He later became known to the English-speaking world as explorer John Cabot. Cabot is credited with being the first European to explore northeastern North America, which he claimed for the British in 1497 (pictured). Five years earlier, another man from Genoa had landed in the southern area of North America. His name was Christopher Columbus.

together through the Union of Utrecht. The Republic of Seven United Netherlands declared their independence from Spain in 1581. These Dutch people embraced their new independence with what was most important to them: political and religious freedom, education, and law and order.

Russell Shorto, a New Netherland researcher, commented on what made the Netherlands different from other European countries: "Maybe the most striking difference between the Netherlands and England was that the new government of the seven united Dutch provinces formed during their struggle was something utterly anomalous [unusual] in Europe: in the midst of the great age of monarchies, stretching from Elizabeth Tudor to Louis XIV, the Dutch carved out a republic."[1]

Instead of a king or queen ruling the Netherlands, this country had elected representatives to manage the government. (After the American Revolution, the United States would also become a republic.)

The Dutch soon dominated the fishing industry of the North Sea. Yet the Netherlands became resentful of Spain's growing hold on the rest of the world. In 1588, the Spanish Armada tried to invade Britain. The British defeated Spain, who later called a truce. Spain no longer controlled all the trade. Afterward, Dutch merchants and sea captains joined forces to seek trade routes to eastern Asia, which they called the Orient. In 1595, the first ship from the Netherlands left for the East. By 1602, the States-General of the Netherlands granted a charter to the East India Company to establish trade routes to Asia and claim any uncharted land. The East India Company became phenomenally successful, particularly in trading the silks and spices found in China and Indonesia.

Interest heightened in finding a northeast route to the Orient. At the time, traders could take the difficult land route over Europe and Asia, or they could sail around the southern tip of Africa. If a northern passage could be found, the journey would be quicker and less treacherous. The East India Company hired a British sea captain named Henry Hudson to find such a route. Hudson was already an experienced explorer of the Arctic. His first two voyages in 1607 and 1608 for England ended when ice blocked his route. He set out on his third voyage in March or April of 1609 in the *Halve Maen* (*Half Moon*) for the Dutch East India Company.

The *Half Moon* was an 85-foot, three-masted Dutch jacht built in 1608. Sixteen crew, Dutch and English seamen, sailed with Hudson. As they sailed along the icy coast of Norway, talks of mutiny may have convinced Hudson to change course. The *Half Moon* probably sailed as far as the Barents Sea near Russia before altering its course to the west. Maybe Hudson could find a northwest route to the Orient. The *Half Moon* reached Newfoundland in the southern part of Canada and sailed south, stopping on the Maine coast to replace a foremast lost in storms.

Hudson sailed south to North Carolina before turning back around. He had seen a few places where the water stretched inland, and he wanted to check them further. He sailed into Delaware Bay to explore it, but turned around when the crew spotted dangerous sandbars that could damage the ship. Hudson continued up the coast. He entered New York Bay on September 3 and decided to explore the wide mouth of a river that seemed to be heading north. Eighty-five years earlier, an

Italian explorer, Giovanni da Verrazano, had been the first European to sail into New York Bay, but he didn't go any farther in exploring the mouth of the river. Hudson hoped the river would eventually veer west, offering a passage through America to Asia. Robert Juet, an English ship's officer traveling on the *Half Moon,* recorded in his journal that the river was full of fish.

Hudson made it as far as present-day Albany before the river became too shallow to continue. He named the river the Mauritus River after Prince Maurice of Nassau in the Netherlands. It became better known as the North River. Years later, the river was renamed the Hudson River in honor of its first European explorer. Hudson claimed the bay and the surrounding region as belonging to the Netherlands.

Hudson explored the coastline and other rivers, including the Delaware River (called the South River by the Dutch). He traded furs with some Indians before leaving the New World.

Hudson sailed one more time, in 1610, once again for the British, and landed in Canada's Hudson Bay. His crew declared mutiny and set him, his teenaged son, and seven crew members adrift. They were never heard from again.

Meanwhile, Dutch merchants were excited about the trade possibilities the New World offered. The English had settled south in Virginia, and the French had claimed eastern Canada (called New France). The wide expanse of land that lay unclaimed between the two presented trade opportunities.

On July 26, 1610, fur trader Arnout Vogels set off for what was probably the first trading expedition in New Netherland. The next year, Vogels sailed on the *Fortuyn* under Captain Adriaen Block. Block sailed around what he thought was a peninsula, but discovered it was a long island. He simply called it *'t Lange Eylandt* (Long Island). He is believed to be the first European to sail into Long Island Sound. He traded guns, clothes, trinkets, and liquor for furs. In making contact with the Indian tribes through trading, he was one of the earliest traders to learn about wampum. Block returned to New Netherland in 1613 on the *Tyger*. His ship caught fire off the coast of Manhattan Island and was destroyed. He spent the winter camping among the Indians and in

On his third voyage to find a northern passage to the Orient, Heny Hudson sailed on the *Half Moon* with sixteen crewman and landed in North America. After exploring the Hudson River, he traded with the Wampanoags, Mohegans, and Quinnipiacs.

the spring built a new ship called the *Onrust*, which means "Restless." The ship was too small to make an ocean voyage, but it was perfect for exploring New Netherland. Block began accurately mapping the land and waterways of the colony. He traveled up and down the Hudson and traded with the Wampanoags, Mohegans, and Quinnipiacs. He became the first European to explore the Connecticut River, which he named the Versche, or Fresh, River. In all, Block charted five river systems. Eventually, he met a larger ship that took him back to the Netherlands. Block made a total of four trips to New Netherland.

The first half of the 1600s was a productive time in Dutch history. In addition to trade and exploration, much progress was made in the arts and sciences. The microscope was invented. The master painter Rembrandt produced some of his greatest works. Amsterdam became one of Europe's leading port cities, and schools and universities of the Netherlands grew. Already leaders in world trade, the Dutch saw the New World as a land of opportunity.

The Dutch had been so successful with the spice trade in the East that they held high hopes for similar financial success in the New World. Historian William Heard Kilpatrick commented, "Over the years the company in the East became increasingly more attractive to the merchants of the Netherlands as a model of what might also be done in the West if a great commercial company could be formed for that area."[2]

Dutch merchants were particularly interested in the fur trade in the New World. Europe had once received many of its furs from Russia. However, the demand for beaver fur exceeded the Russian supply. From the reports of Adriaen Block and others, furs were abundant in this new land. On October 11, 1614, the governing body of the Netherlands, the States-General of the United Provinces, granted a three-year monopoly on fur trading in New Netherland to a group of private merchants. This was the first time the name *New Netherland* appeared in a legal document.

In late 1614 or early 1615, Dutch fur traders built a fort on the North (Hudson) River at what they knew to be a good fur trading area. They built the fort on Castle Island, a few miles south of where the Mohawk River joins the Hudson. The traders named it Fort Nassau after the house of Orange-Nassau, the noble family of the Netherlands. They soon found out that the island flooded each spring. It was abandoned in 1618. Today, it is underwater.

The States-General did not renew the monopoly at the end of the three-year period, but instead opened the area to other merchants. Meanwhile, the Dutch East India Company continued to profit from trading in Asia. One merchant, William Usselinx, suggested the formation of a Dutch *West* India Company to explore and trade in the New World.

The merchants and government of the Netherlands wanted to conquer a new land and meet new challenges. Agreeing with Usselinx, they decided to focus their efforts on New Netherland through the formation of a new West India Company.

The Hudson River

The Hudson River is named after Henry Hudson, the first European to explore the river. At 306 miles (492 km) long, the Hudson River flows through the state of New York on its way to the Atlantic Ocean. For the last 21 miles (34 km), it marks the border between New York and New Jersey before ending in New York Harbor.

The river begins high above sea level in the Adirondack Mountains, with rapids and waterfalls that were used to power textile mills in the 1800s. Near Troy, New York, north of Albany, the river enters a valley created long ago by glaciers. During the American Revolution, more battles were fought in New York than any other colony, with the Hudson River Valley particularly desired by both sides, who wanted to use the river to transport troops and supplies.

The river then runs through New York's capital, Albany, where it widens and drops below sea level. About fifty miles north of New York City, the hills along the river rise up more than a thousand feet on both shores, and strong currents made navigating the fifteen-mile stretch difficult. Dutch sailors nicknamed this section of the river World's End or the Devil's Horse Race. It took experienced navigators to sail ocean ships from the Atlantic Ocean to Albany without difficulty.

In the 1800s, there was a great need to reach the interior states for trade. Work started in 1817 on the 363-mile (584-km) Erie

Stony Point Lighthouse

Canal to connect the Hudson River to Lake Erie. In 1825, the Erie Canal was completed and became a gateway to the west as ships could finally travel from the Atlantic Ocean to the Great Lakes. This opened the area for further trade, and New York City became a leading port. Because of the increased traffic on the Hudson, a system of lighthouses was built, the first being the octagonal Stony Point Lighthouse in 1826. The number of lighthouses grew to fourteen; only seven remain today.

As the second director-general, or governor, of New Netherland, Peter Minuit (center) is best known for his trades with the Lenni Lenape (Delaware) tribe. He traded trinkets worth approximately $24 for Manhattan Island. Minuit later bought Staten Island for tools, duffels, and wampum.

Chapter

3

Colonizing New Netherland

The West India Company was established in 1621, with offices on Brewer Street in Amsterdam. The government awarded the company a charter with a twenty-four-year trading monopoly in the Americas and Africa, yet the government would oversee the West India Company and the settlements. A board representing the different regions in the Netherlands appointed Willem Verhulst as director-general, or governor, of the new Dutch province of New Netherland. The role of the director-general in New Netherlands was vague, but focused on seeing to the interests of the Dutch West India Company, often referred to as the Company. A succession of five directors-general would govern the province of New Netherland while it was under Dutch rule.

More than anything, the West India Company was about making a profit. According to the charter: "The managers of this Company shall solemnly promise and swear, that they will act well and faithfully in their administration, and make good and just accounts of their trade."[1] Much of the charter reflects the importance of running a profitable business and distributing the profits equally among the shareholders.

The company began settling the colony of New Netherland. Fifty-two families had arrived by spring of 1624: those on the *Unity*, and another group two months later on the *New Netherland*. These families were the first people the company paid to colonize the area. Six additional ships brought more colonists and supplies that year and the next. Both peasants and the wealthy arrived. Many settlers worked for the company, but doctors, midwives, craftsmen, surveyors, and farmers were also among the group.

Director-general Verhulst arrived in 1625 with instructions to strengthen the trading posts. He was also instructed to treat the Indians fairly, yet not interfere in intertribal affairs. Although the Dutch settlers often traded with the Iroquois and Algonquin tribes, the northern and southern settlements had to be abandoned by 1626 as unlivable. Part of the reason were attacks by the Mohawk tribe. The company paid soldiers to protect the colonists. The soldiers of Fort Orange aligned themselves with the small village of Mahicans (enemies of the Mohawks) on the east side of the river, thus not paying attention to the rule to not become involved in tribal affairs. The Mohawks attacked a Mahican party and killed twenty-four Mahicans, three soldiers, plus fort commander Daniel van Crieckenbeeck. Many settlers moved from Fort Orange to New Amsterdam after the attack. Initially, they stayed in Fort Amsterdam, which was the hub of all settlements at this time. Company soldiers lived at the fort, which was also the site of council sessions. The settlers knew that Fort Amsterdam was the safest place to go when there was an attack.

Verhulst apparently was not a good leader. Concerned about safety and the leadership, the settlers formed a committee that voted to banish Verhulst from New Netherland. Rumors that he cheated the settlers and the Indians came to the attention of the company. Peter Minuit had arrived with an early group of settlers as a scout for the West India Company. The settlers were familiar with Minuit and in 1626 voted him as the new director-general.

As the second director-general, one of Minuit's first acts was to purchase Manhattan Island—probably from the Lenni Lenape (Delaware) tribe—for trinkets worth sixty guilders (approximately $24). The Lenni Lenape planned to continue using Manhattan Island and may have hoped the transaction would make these Dutch people their allies against the Iroquois. There is no known written deed in existence, only references to this transaction in letters of the time. This purchase was similar to other purchases between Europeans and native tribes of the area. Minuit bought Staten Island in 1630 from another Delaware tribe, the Tappans, for items like duffels, tools, and wampum. Other land along the Hudson and Delaware Rivers was traded for similar items, including glass beads.

Soon after the purchase of Manhattan, Minuit began building the city of New Amsterdam, which would become the most important area of New Netherland. (Today, New Amsterdam is known as New York City, the largest city in the United States.) The year New Amsterdam was founded, thirty houses were built. A church, city hall, and taverns also went up. The West India Company instructed that several large farms or *bouweries* should also be included. The largest bowery was for the use of the director-general of the colony.

The first settlers lived in sod or pit houses, made from large pits dug in the earth. Wood covered the floors and walls, while the roofs were made of sod or bark. Soon, the settlers built homes from stone, brick, and wood. Many Dutch homes had one and a half stories or more. They faced south in order to take advantage of the sun. A steep roof covered the house and came close to the ground on the north side. Doors to the outside, known as Dutch doors, had an upper half and a lower half. This allowed a person to talk to others through the open upper half while the closed lower half kept out farm animals. Fireplaces provided heat, light, and places to cook. Wealthy Dutch colonists brought furniture, wall hangings, and blue-and-white-glazed pottery called delftware with them to the new land. In Long Island homes, housewives or servants might make homes more decorative by creating temporary geometric patterns in the sand floors.

However, a few short years later, some colonists began returning to the Netherlands, finding the life of a settler too difficult. By 1630, about three hundred people lived in New Netherland. About thirty had returned to Fort Orange (Albany), which was the center of the fur trade. The remainder were spread out on individual farms throughout New Netherland, many of which surrounded New Amsterdam.

The West India Company had trouble increasing the numbers of settlers. Few Dutch people wanted to leave the Netherlands, where so many opportunities in business, art, and education existed. The company had more success in drawing settlers from other European countries, such as Finland, Sweden, Germany, and England. At least eighteen languages were used in New Netherland in the 1600s.

The West India Company began having some success when it enacted the Charter of Freedoms and Exemptions of 1629. Also known as the patroonship plan, this act permitted wealthy individuals to establish personal estates in New Netherland. Property owners called patroons were given a large acreage of land on the condition that they would bring fifty settlers. The settlers would be tenants under the patroon. Much like the lord of an estate, the patroon had the power to settle minor disagreements among people living in their area. The plan gave five patroons the right to trade in furs and fish along the Hudson River between Fort Orange and Fort Amsterdam. One of the patroons along the Hudson River was a shareholder in the West India Company named Kiliaen van Rensselaer. His estate of Rensselaerswyck soon became the largest and most financially successful fur trading area.

New Netherland never became as successful a venture as the West India Company had hoped. Not as profitable as its East India counterpart, the West India Company may have spread its resources too thin. The East India Company focused primarily on the spice trade in the Orient and opening up trade centers in foreign ports like Java in Indonesia. The West India Company began colonies not only in North America, but also in Africa, South America, and the Caribbean. The Dutch had an ongoing battle with the Portuguese over claims in Brazil. They also fought with the Spanish to keep possession of the Netherlands Antilles, which included Curaçao, Aruba, and St. Martin.

"Dutch global expansion during its century of empire was built around not settlement colonies but outposts, which explains why, even though the empire extended as far afield as India, Taiwan, and Java, the Dutch language is not spread around the globe the way English is,"[2] explains Shortos.

In New Netherland, the fur trade was most important. Dutch merchants had established trading posts in order to trade with the Indians. Beaver fur was especially desired by the merchants. On December 28, 1630, the New Netherland government adopted a seal

In the 17th century, the Dutch had colonies and trading posts all over the world, including New Netherland, the Netherlands Antilles, Brazil, South Africa, Iran, India, Indonesia, and Taiwan. Trading was conducted either by the Dutch East India Company or by the less successful Dutch West India Company.

for use on legal documents. The seal showed a beaver on a small shield. Beavers symbolized wealth to the Dutch.

The traders became aware of wampum, which had been used in trading among the inland and coastal tribes. The Pequot tribe polished pieces of clam or whelk shells, which came from Long Island. They turned the tiny purple and white shells into beads by piercing them with a hole so that they could be strung. These beads were wampum. The Mohawks highly prized wampum, particularly the dark beads. The Dutch traded goods like cookware for the wampum. Then they traded wampum for beaver skins, which they used to make coats and hats. Using wampum gave the Dutch an edge in trading.

According to historian Kevin McBride, "Although the Dutch were not the first Europeans in the region, they were the first to develop and sustain long-term trade with native populations and the first to have a detectable impact on the native culture."[3]

Even with the wealth generated by trade, the costs of settlement came high. The company had a business relationship with the settlers. Craftsmen were often paid employees. The company provided farmers with land and livestock. The farmers then paid the company one tenth of their crops for the first ten years.

"The acquisition of furs in New Netherland was the primary activity throughout the period of Dutch trade (ca 1610–1664), but furs were largely depleted in coastal regions of New Netherland within a decade of the establishment of the Dutch West India Company in 1621,"[4] according to McBride.

Concerned about the lack of settlement, the board of the West India Company blamed Minuit and fired him in 1631. Furious, Minuit would later lead a group of Swedes to America and found New Sweden (which would become Wilmington, Delaware).

Minuit was replaced by Wouter van Twiller. Previously a young clerk in the West India Company office, Van Twiller wasn't prepared to be a leader. Instead he was described as a drunk with poor judgment. On one occasion, a British ship captain demanded to be allowed to go up the North River to trade with the Indians, and, against regulations, Van Twiller allowed it.

By 1638, the company began opening trade in areas other than fur to any merchant willing to pay a fee. Legal conditions were described in the Articles and Conditions of 1638. Merchants from other countries could trade if they agreed to pay a 10 percent import fee and a 15 percent export fee. Additionally, they had to use company ships to transport goods.

The first merchants to take advantage of these new laws were former West India Company merchants. Some Dutch merchants traded on behalf of large firms. In the end, a few Dutch merchants controlled most of the New Netherland trade.

Meanwhile, New Amsterdam became more unruly. Barroom fights were common in the increasing number of taverns and breweries there. New Netherland desperately needed a strong leader, and Van Twiller wasn't it. Would the fourth director-general, Willem Kieft, be the one who could restore order?

Native Americans

When the Dutch and other Europeans arrived in America, they were met by people from many native tribes. Some were friendly to the travelers and engaged in trade with them. According to historians, two linguistic groups of tribes lived in the New Netherland area. The Algonquin people, who lived in southern New York along the ocean, were a loosely organized group that included the Delaware, Mahican, Montauk, Munsee, and others. It was the Delaware word *Mahattos*, meaning "hilly island," that was used by the settlers for the island that would later be called Manhattan. The Algonquins made the wampum for which the other groups traded.

A modern painting of Hiawatha

The Iroquois, on the other hand, were a very well organized confederacy and a formidable opponent in battle. Once, the Iroquois fought among themselves. During the 1300s, these Iroquois tribes decided to put aside their differences and formed the powerful Iroquois Confederacy. It was one of the first known democracies. One of the men who helped create the confederacy was a Mohawk man named Hiawatha.

The five main tribes of the Iroquois were the Mohawk, Oneida, Onondaga, Cayuga, and Seneca. The Tuscaroras joined later. The Iroquois called themselves the Haudenosaunee, which means "People Building a Long House." The traditional home of the Iroquois was a long house in which a clan of as many as twenty related families lived.

The Algonquins and Iroquois had not only different languages, but also different backgrounds and customs. They had been fighting intermittently since before Hudson's exploratory voyage. The arrival of the Europeans deepened their differences.

A good relationship with all the tribes was necessary to the goals of the Dutch West India Company. The most valuable item to the Dutch merchants was furs, and it was the Native Americans who provided them. Therefore, the company required that all dealings with the Indians be done honestly. Director-general Peter Stuyvesant reportedly publicly punished a woman who was found guilty of cheating Indians with whom she had traded.

FYI For Your Information

Peter Stuyvesant was the fifth and last director-general of New Netherland. After losing his leg in a battle for the Caribbean Island of St. Martin, he was appointed to his last post in New Netherland. He was a firm leader who instituted a court of justice and advisory committees. He was involved in boundary disputes with neighboring colonies and forcibly took over New Sweden.

Chapter

(4)

Territory Disputes

The son of a merchant, Willem Kieft, who arrived in New Netherland in 1638, was also a businessman. He realized it wasn't good business for New Netherland when Peter Minuit created the colony of New Sweden at the border of New Netherland. Now New Netherland merchants and traders had new competition.

As a business, New Netherland was floundering and in need of funds. Kieft thought he could raise money by taxing the Indians for services the colonists provided. Although the settlers tried to tell Kieft that this was a bad idea, he refused to listen. When the tribes did not pay the tax, Kieft began punishing them for incidents that had previously been ignored. When hogs were stolen from a farm on Staten Island, he had some Indians killed. Other members of the tribe retaliated by burning down the farm and killing farm hands. Kieft then began setting tribes against one another.

When a young Wickquasgeck Indian avenged the murder of his family, Kieft waged war on the entire tribe. Soldiers massacred a village. Tribes turned around and destroyed Dutch homes. After several years of sporadic fighting, Kieft was ordered to arrange for a peace treaty.

Willem Kieft (in red) plots with Dutch colleagues against the Indians. Kieft's War, which would last from 1643 to 1645, would claim the lives of at least 1,000 Indians. When Peter Stuyvesant replaced Kieft as director-general in 1647, Kieft boarded a ship for home. He never made it back to the Netherlands, but was lost at sea.

In 1647, Petrus (Peter) Stuyvesant was chosen to be the fifth director-general of New Netherland. From the moment he stepped off the boat, he made it clear that he was a different sort of leader. Historian Russell Shorto describes his arrival: "In his remark, Stuyvesant vowed to act 'like a father over his children.' His signals of power were clear-cut: While the men of the community had removed their hats in his honor, he kept his on. While the colonists remained standing, he took a chair."[1]

Stuyvesant took charge immediately. When a drunken knife fight broke out on a Sunday afternoon, he forbade taverns from selling alcohol until 2:00 P.M. He also let it be known that anyone drawing a knife in passion or anger would face six months' jail time.

Meanwhile, disagreements arose concerning a range of issues, from religion to borders. Although the Dutch West India Company's policy of religious tolerance was the same as in the Netherlands, Peter Stuyvesant didn't agree. The son of a Calvinist minister, Stuyvesant did not support diversity. When the Reformed Dutch Church ministers asked him to stop Lutherans from worshiping, he declared that they couldn't worship in public. After the Netherlands lost Brazil to the Portuguese in 1654, about twenty-three to thirty Jewish people came from Brazil to New Netherland. Stuyvesant had them jailed and then expelled. The Jewish people appealed to the West India Company, who, with Jewish stockholders, overturned Stuyvesant's decision. When Stuyvesant tried to expel the Society of Friends (Quakers) from the town of Flushing on Long Island, an interesting thing happened. The colonists banded together against Stuyvesant to say that all should be allowed to worship as they wished. Called the Flushing Remonstrance, this incident was an early sign of the freedoms for which the settlers were willing to fight.

The borders of New Netherland had long been vague. The Dutch considered the Fresh (Connecticut) River to be the northern border. Therefore, part of present-day Connecticut was part of New Netherland. Historians claim that because there are many Dutch place-names in Connecticut, such as Saybrook and Greenwich, the Dutch influence there was great.

The southern border was the South (Delaware) River, which provided the company with all of New Jersey and some of Delaware. Trading centers were created in Wilmington, Delaware, and in Trenton and Newark, New Jersey.

Even with the other trading posts, New Amsterdam remained the center of New Netherland activity. Stuyvesant created a nearby settlement for "lovers of agriculture." The new settlement, called New Haarlem, was located at the northern end of Manhattan Island. Settlers received 36 to 45 acres of arable land and 12 to 16 acres of meadowland.

By 1655, the Swedish West India Company had operated New Sweden (founded by Peter Minuit) for seventeen years in Delaware and part of New Jersey. Stuyvesant sailed up the Delaware River with seven warships and 350 soldiers, defeating New Sweden and taking over Fort Christina (Wilmington). He renamed the territory New Amstel. The Swedes who remained became citizens of New Netherland.

However, the main enemy of New Netherland was consistently the British. From 1640 to 1660, England had been engaged in a civil war and did not have a king. Although not actively involved in colonization during this time, many British citizens came to the New World to escape the war and religious persecution. Furthermore, some British colonists were unhappy with the Puritan government of the Massachusetts Bay and Plymouth colonies to the north. Since 1630, increasing numbers of British lived in or near New Netherland, primarily along the New York–Connecticut border or on Long Island. Of the Long Island villages surrounding New Amsterdam, about half were English and the other half, including Breuckelen (Brooklyn), were Dutch.

As early as 1633, England claimed to own the Connecticut River, based on John Cabot's 1497 voyage in the service of England. The Dutch were fewer and more spread out and decided to focus their efforts on keeping New Amsterdam and settlements north to Fort Orange. The Treaty of Hartford in 1650 divided Long Island at the town of Oyster Bay. The Dutch owned the western part and the British had the east. Connecticut was likewise divided between Greenwich (Dutch controlled) and Stanford (British controlled). The city of Hartford was British, but the Dutch were allowed to keep a fort there.

Adriaen van der Donck, also known as Colen van der Donck, came to New Netherland as a young lawyer in 1641 intent on establishing much-needed law and order to the colony. He believed that the citizens of New Netherland should be treated with the same rights as the citizens in the homeland. Both Kieft and Stuyvesant disagreed with him. Van der Donck wrote to the Dutch government about New Netherland and New Amsterdam. He persuaded the government of the Netherlands to give New Amsterdam a charter. New Amsterdam became an official city on February 2, 1653. The residents quickly elected their officials, including two co-mayors and a team of judges.

Increasing problems with the British led the colonists of New Amsterdam to build a wall across lower Manhattan for protection against a possible invasion. The logs for the wall were twelve feet high by eighteen inches wide. Built in 1653, the wall stretched from the East River straight across to the Hudson River. The wall was never used for defense, but it gave its name to Wall Street, a place where brokers would

Increasing conflicts with the British led Dutch colonists to build a wall across Manhattan in case of a possible invasion. The wall was never used and came down several years later. People remember the wall, however, in the name of Wall Street.

trade stocks, and which would much later become the financial center of the United States.

Ongoing conflicts with the British led to three Anglo-Dutch wars during the seventeenth century. The British instituted the Navigation Acts of 1651, which prohibited non-English ships from transporting goods from English ports. Because Dutch merchants traded a fair amount in both Britain and the British colonies of New England and Virginia, this law heavily impacted the Netherlands, which until that time had been successful in trade ventures. On July 6, 1652, the

Charles II (left) became Britain's king in 1660. He had a difficult rule that included wars with other European countries and the plague in his own country. He declared New Netherland a British province, which he gave to his brother, James II (right). Upon the death of Charles in 1685, James II became king.

Netherlands declared war on Britain over trading rights and land ownership. They called a truce in 1654, ending the first Anglo-Dutch War.

Charles II assumed the British throne in 1660. The new king annexed New Netherland as a British province in March 1664 and gave it to this brother, James, the Duke of York. British warships were sent to seize control of New Netherland. Director-general Stuyvesant would have preferred to fight, but the Dutch colonists were too few and refused to take up arms. Stuyvesant had no choice but to surrender to the British on September 8, 1664.

Religion and Education

When the Dutch people liberated the Netherlands from Spanish oppression in 1581, they embraced religious freedom and became known throughout Europe as the most tolerant of different religions. Spanish Catholicism was allowed, but the official religion of the Netherlands became the Reformed Dutch Church. People from other countries who were being persecuted moved to the Netherlands. Many of these same people later moved to New Netherland.

Dutch Reformed Church

The first church service in New Netherland was held at Fort Orange in 1624, although it would be another year before the first minister arrived. By the time the British took over New Netherland in 1664, six ministers of the Reformed Dutch Church served the colony.

In Dutch society, churches and schools often worked together. All elementary education was done through parochial or church-sponsored schools. When Dutch settlers moved to New Netherland, they continued to allow the church to handle education. Boys and girls both attended school, but separately.

The first school in New Netherland was established in the 1630s. Adam Roelantsen is documented as being the first licensed teacher in 1637. It was normal practice to license teachers after they passed an examination that tested their "moral fitness." However, it is possible that New Netherland had schools with unlicensed teachers as early as 1633.

Schools introduced reading, writing, basic math, Dutch history, and religion. More math was taught in New Netherland because of the importance of commerce and trade. Students who continued in their studies past eighth grade often went to Latin schools to study Latin and Greek.

Children attended school year round, although farming communities often had the school year scheduled around planting and harvest. While the teacher had a desk and chair, the students usually sat on benches, with the oldest boys sitting in front. An average school day was held in two sessions, from eight to eleven in the morning, then, after a break, from one to four. Children often attended school six days a week.

The New Amsterdam City School was one of the best-known schools in the colony. Even during British possession, it continued as a Dutch school, eventually becoming New York City School.

When the British warships arrived to take over New Netherland in 1664, the Dutch colonists refused to fight. The British and the Dutch met over the terms of surrender which became known as the Articles of Capitulation on the Reduction New Netherland. The terms were quite generous to the Dutch colonists and allowed them to continue much as they had before.

Chapter

5

New Netherland Lives On

When Peter Stuyvesant surrendered to the British in 1664, he did so with very lenient terms written by a committee of members from both sides. The terms were called the Articles of Capitulation on the Reduction of New Netherland. Two of the twenty-three terms in the agreement stated:

> All people shall still continue as free denizens and enjoy the lands, house, goods, ships, wheresoever they are within the country, and dispose of them as they please. (Article 3)
>   The Dutch here shall enjoy their own customs concerning their inheritances. (Article 11)[1]

These articles were so successful that they continued to be used as New Netherland changed hands a few more times. They were also used when America drafted its Bill of Rights over a hundred years later.

Although Governor Peter Stuyvesant wanted to fight the British, the colonists wanted to live peacefully. Stuyvesant accepted the surrender terms, an incident which earned him a reprimand from the Dutch West India Company.

A second Anglo-Dutch war began in 1664 when the British captured New Amsterdam in peacetime. It ended on July 31, 1667, with the Treaty of Breda. In the treaty, the Netherlands gave up rights to New Netherland in exchange for Suriname in South America. Peace didn't last long, though. England and France joined forces in 1672 to assume control of the Netherlands, starting the third Anglo-Dutch war. The European war carried over into North America. In the summer of 1673, a fleet of Dutch ships belonging to Jacob Benckes and Cornelis Evertsz captured or destroyed ships carrying Virginia tobacco. The next month, Captain Anthony Colve sailed into the Hudson River with 600 Dutch soldiers. They attacked Fort James (which had been Fort Amsterdam). They regained control of the fort on August 9. They jailed the British governor, Francis Lovelace. After taking control of New York City and renaming it New Orange, the soldiers proceeded to take other settlements, including Albany (renamed Willemstad) and New Jersey.

Dutch rule was much briefer this time, lasting less than a year. The British resumed control of the North American colonies on February 9, 1674, with the signing of the Treaty of Westminster. The Articles of Capitulation were reinstated. When the new British governor, Major Edmund Andros, arrived in New York City, he gave the Dutch one week to leave. Dutch governor Colve persuaded Andros to agree to eleven more articles, outlining agreements from religious freedom to property rights for the settlers. Place-names were changed back. New Netherland once again became New York, and New Amsterdam became New York City. But little else changed for the Dutch settlers.

According to historian William Heard Kilpatrick, the Dutch schools and households were little affected by the change in government. "For a long time after the English took over the colony, the Dutch clung to their language and customs."[2]

Meanwhile, in England, the Duke of York had become King James II. A Catholic, King James II upset the British with his attempts to appoint Roman Catholics to political and military positions. Dutch leader Willem III Hendrick, Prince of Orange, Stadhouder of Holland and Zeeland, was welcomed by the British when he invaded the southwest coast of England with 21,000 troops. His wife, Mary, was the eldest daughter of James II and his first wife, Anne Hyde, a Protestant. Willem and Mary continued on to London, where they assumed the British throne in 1688 as King William III and Queen Mary II.

The frequent changing of governing power did not affect the settlers strongly, in part because of the articles first established in 1664. Altercations were mostly limited to the sea or forts. Buildings and homes weren't burned or destroyed. The English, Germans, Swedes, Finns, French, and Dutch cooperated with one another. Eventually the colonists ceased to be identified by their country of origin, but by the country they now called home. They were Americans.

According to Dutch colonial expert Maud Esther Dilliard, "Although Dutch rule there was ended forever, Dutch influence would last for generations."[3] People spoke Dutch and built Dutch homes into the 1800s. Dutch place-names have lived even longer. *'T Lang Eylandt* became Long Island. *Breuckelen* was Brooklyn. *New Haarlem* became a neighborhood in Manhattan called Harlem. *Staten Eylandt* (Staten Island) took its name from the States-General who governed the Netherlands in the early 1600s. Dutch place-names and family names continue to be found throughout the northeastern United States.

Many skilled craftsmen, including cabinet makers and silver-smiths, settled in New Netherland. In 1809 a writer named Washington Irving retold legends from New Netherland. Using the pen name Diedrich Knickerbocker, Irving wrote a satirical work, *A History of New York*, in which he portrayed Peter Stuyvesant as a tyrant.

One tradition started by the Dutch was Sinterklaas, the celebration each year of the birthday of St. Nicolaas on December 5 by giving presents to children. In English, the gentleman is better known as Santa Claus.

After losing New Netherland to the British and some holdings in the West Indies to the French, the Dutch West India Company operated primarily in Africa until its charter expired in 1791. After the French invasion of the Netherlands in 1794, the West India Company was dissolved, but to be Dutch remained something to be proud of in New Netherland. "There was a saying among those who had dealings with them in the mid-nineteenth century that a Dutchman's word was as good as his bond,"[4] claims Dilliard.

When people first came to America from the Netherlands, they were drawn to a valley bordering a river and a forested island on the Atlantic Ocean. Both locations, the Hudson River Valley and Manhattan, are of significant importance to the United States of today.

New information about the beginnings of New Netherland and the Dutch influence comes to light every day. The secretary of New Netherland kept his office and papers in Fort Amsterdam. These papers were moved to a vault in the New York State Library in Albany. A project called the New Netherland Project has been translating and publishing the papers.

The center of Dutch colonial life, New Amsterdam, became New York City after the British took over. New York City continued to grow, becoming the largest city in the United States. In later years, immigrants who arrived in New York City were greeted by the Statue of Liberty on Liberty Island.

When the Europeans began colonizing the United States, the Dutch were a large part of the settlement and history. Long before there were thirteen colonies, there was New Netherland, which had a lasting impact. The founding of New Netherland introduced many of the attributes that the Bill of Rights of the United States was founded upon—ultimately, life, liberty, and the pursuit of happiness.

Peter Stuyvesant

Petrus, or Peter Stuyvesant, was the last, and probably best known, of the five directors-general of New Netherland. He also served the longest, after following a series of inept directors-general. Stuyvesant was an intelligent and efficient leader, yet his periods of bad temper made him unpopular with many colonists.

Stuyvesant was born sometime between 1601 and 1610 in Scherpenzeel, Friesland, of the Netherlands. After attending the University of Franeker, he joined the Dutch West India Company in 1632. Three years later he left for South America. In 1643, he was selected as director-general of Curaçao, Aruba, and Bonaire in the Caribbean. When trying to capture the Spanish Island of St. Martin, he was injured and lost his leg.

While visiting his sister, he met her sister-in-law, Judith Bayard. Judith and Peter were married in a Walloon church on August 13, 1645.

In 1647, New Netherland was added to the provinces over which Stuyvesant would be director-general. He arrived in Manhattan on the *Princess* with his wife and his widowed sister. He was a formidable sight, with his wooden leg and stern manner. As director-general, he governed the colonists and negotiated treaties with the Native Americans. Much of his rule was spent in disputes with other European countries. The Netherlands and Britain were often at odds as to what constituted their respective colonies.

In 1664, when the British ordered the surrender of New Netherland and the colonists refused to fight, Stuyvesant was summoned to speak to the board of the Dutch West India

Peter Stuyvesant waving his cane in New Amsterdam

Company. He had to explain why he had surrendered without a single shot being fired. Disgusted, Stuyvesant returned to New Netherland as a private citizen to settle on his New Amsterdam farm, Bowery Number One, which he had purchased from the West India Company twenty years earlier. Stuyvesant died there in 1672 and lies buried at the family chapel, which later became the Church of St. Marks-in-the-Bowery.

Chapter Notes

Chapter 1
Voyage to a New Land

1. This chapter is based on testimonies Catelina Rapalje provided at ages 80 and 83. She and her husband were definitely on the first ship that brought colonists to New Netherland. Catelina Rapalje testified that she and the first group of colonists sailed on the *Eendracht* (*Unity*), arriving in 1623 or 1624. However, none of the accounts from the West India Company mentions a ship called the *Eendracht*—although the company does mention the ship *Nieuw Nederlandt* (*New Netherland*). There is no confirmation of the exact number of colonists that arrived in the first or second ship to New Netherland. Pierre may have been a passenger on the first ship with his parents, Jean and Jacqueline Monfort, and any siblings.

Chapter 2
New Netherland Discovered

1. Russell Shorto, *The Island at the Center of the World: The Epic Story of Dutch Manhattan and the Forgotten Colony That Shaped America* (New York: Doubleday, 2004), p. 27.

2. William Heard Kilpatrick, *The Dutch Schools of New Netherland and Colonial New York* (New York: Arno Press and the New York Times, 1969), p. 50.

Chapter 3
Colonizing New Netherland

1. New Netherland Project: Charter of the Dutch West India Company, **http://www.nnp.org/newvtour/xpages/wic.html**

2. Russell Shorto, *The Island at the Center of the World: The Epic Story of Dutch Manhattan and the Forgotten Colony That Shaped America* (New York: Doubleday, 2004), p. 113.

3. Laurie Weinstein (editor), *Enduring Traditions: The Native Peoples of New England* (Westport, CT: Cergin & Garvey, 1994), p. 33.

4. Ibid., p. 31.

Chapter 4
Territory Disputes

1 Russell Shorto, *The Island at the Center of the World: The Epic Story of Dutch Manhattan and the Forgotten Colony That Shaped America* (New York: Doubleday, 2004), p. 167.

Chapter 5
New Netherland Lives On

1. New Netherland Museum and the *Half Moon* "Articles of Capitulation on the Reduction of New Netherland" [General Entries, I., 1664–1665, p. 23, In Secretary of State's Office, Albany, N.Y.] **http://www.newnetherland.org/history.html#AoC**

2. William Heard Kilpatrick, *The Dutch Schools of New Netherland and Colonial New York* (New York: Arno Press and the New York Times, 1969), p. 9.

3. Maud Esther Dilliard, *An Album of New Netherland: Dutch Colonial Antiques and Architecture* (New York: Bramhall House, 1963), p. 14.

4. Ibid., p. 37.

Chronology

1602	Dutch East India Company is chartered by the States-General of the United Provinces.
1609	Henry Hudson explores from Delaware Bay to the upper Hudson as far as present-day Albany on behalf of East India Company.
1614	The New Netherland Company is formed and is given a monopoly on the fur trade in the colony. Fort Nassau is established as a fur trading post on Castle Island, near present-day Albany.
1617	The New Netherland Company's monopoly is not renewed; land is opened to all Dutch traders.
1621	Dutch West India company is incorporated; it establishes a trading monopoly.
1624	First colonists arrive in New Netherland.
1625	Willem Verhulst arrives as first director-general of New Netherland.
1626	Daniel van Crieckenbeeck, commander at Fort Orange, is killed while supporting a Mahican war party against the Mohawks. Peter Minuit replaces Verhulst as director-general; he purchases Manhattan Island.
1629	"Charter of Freedoms and Exemptions" establishes the patroonship plan of colonization.
1630	Minuit buys Staten Island from a Delaware tribe.
1633–1638	Wouter van Twiller is director-general of New Netherland.
1638	Dutch West India Company gives up its trading monopoly, intending to collect fees instead. Peter Minuit establishes New Sweden on the Delaware River. Willem Kieft is director-general of New Netherland; he serves until 1647.
1643–1645	War is waged between Kieft and the Indians around Manhattan Island.
1647	Petrus (Peter) Stuyvesant becomes director-general of New Netherland, Curaçao, and other dependencies in the Caribbean.
1650	Hartford Treaty establishes boundaries between New Netherland and New England.
1651	England's Navigation Acts make it illegal for non-English ships to carry goods from English ports.
1652–1654	First Anglo-Dutch War is fought.
1655	Stuyvesant conquers New Sweden (Wilmington, Delaware).
1664	Stuyvesant surrenders New Netherland to the British.
1664–1667	Second Anglo-Dutch War is fought.
1672–1674	Third Anglo-Dutch War is fought.
1674	New Netherland becomes New York again as a result of the Peace of Westminster.

Timeline in History

1492	Christopher Columbus, sailing for Spain, reaches America.
1497	John Cabot, a Venetian sailing for England, reaches Canada.
1524	Giovanni da Verrazano sails into New York Bay.
1565	St. Augustine, Florida, becomes the first permanent European town in what will be the United States.
1568	Dutch revolt against Spain begins.
1580	Philip II becomes king of Spain and Portugal, uniting these countries.
1579	Willem I, prince of Orange-Nassau, becomes first stadholder.
1584	Willem I is assassinated at his home in Delft.
1588	Spanish Armada is defeated by British Navy.
1602	United East India Company is chartered by the States-General of the United Provinces.
1607	Jamestown colony is established as the first British colony in the Americas.
1620	Pilgrims found Plymouth Colony.
1625	Prince Frederik Hendrik becomes stadholder; he serves until 1647.
1682	Philadelphia is settled.
1706	Benjamin Franklin is born.
1754	The French and Indian War begins.
1776	The Revolutionary War begins.

Further Reading

For Young Adults

Fradin, Dennis B. *The New York Colony*. Chicago: Children's Press, 1988.

Krizner, L.J., and Lisa Sita. *Peter Stuyvesant: New Amsterdam and the Origins of New York*. New York: Rosen Publishing Group, 2001.

Works Consulted

Dilliard, Maud Esther. *An Album of New Netherland: Dutch Colonial Antiques and Architecture*. New York: Bramhall House, 1963.

Kilpatrick, William Heard. *The Dutch Schools of New Netherland and Colonial New York*. New York: Arno Press and the New York Times, 1969.

Shorto, Russell. *The Island at the Center of the World: The Epic Story of Dutch Manhattan and the Forgotten Colony That Shaped America*. New York: Doubleday, 2004.

van Laer, A.J.F. *Annals of New Netherlands*. Edited and annotated by Dr. Charles T. Gehring, Director, New Netherland Project. Albany, NY, 1999.

Weinstein, Laurie (editor). *Enduring Traditions: The Native Peoples of New England*. Westport, Connecticut: Cergin & Garvey, 1994.

On the Internet

"Charter of the Dutch West India Company: 1621"
http://www.nnp.org/newvtour/xpages/wic.html

Department of Special Collections, University of Notre Dame: "A Brief Outline of the History of New Netherland"
http://www.coins.nd.edu/ColCoin/ColCoinIntros/NNHistory.html

Haudenosaunee, People Building a Long House.
http://www.sixnations.org/

Historic Hudson Valley
http://www.hudsonvalley.org/

New Netherland Museum and the *Half Moon*
http://www.newnetherland.org/

New Netherland Project
http://www.nnp.org/

University at Albany: "Early Albany: A Dutch Settlement"
http://www.albany.edu/faculty/mackey/isp523/project/wolf/

"U.S. Towns and Cities with Dutch Names," Netherlands Embassy, Washington, D.C.
http://www.netherlands-embassy.org/article.asp?articleref=AR00000382EN

Glossary

annex
(AA-neks)
For one country to take control of another.

bowery
(BAU-ree)
A Dutch colonial farm; in Dutch, it is spelled *bouwery*.

charter
(CHAR-tur)
A formal document that states the rights or duties of a group of people.

colony
(KAH-luh-nee)
A large group of people settling in new land, but still ruled by leaders of their previous land.

denizens
(DEH-nih-zens)
Inhabitants.

flax
(FLAKS)
The fiber of a specific plant that can be woven into thread and used to make linen.

hull
(HUL)
The frame or body of a boat or ship.

Iroquois
(EER-uh-koi)
A member of a confederation of American Indian tribes originally from New York.

melting pot
A place where people of different cultures or races form an integrated society.

monopoly
(muh-NAA-puh-lee)
The complete control of something, particularly a service or supply of a product.

patroonship
(puh-TROON-ship)
The system whereby people in New Netherland were granted a large tract of land in exchange for bringing fifty new settlers to the colony.

satirical
(suh-TEE-rih-kul)
A written work that subtly makes fun of people and society.

stadholder
(STAD-hoh-der)
A provincial executive officer in the Netherlands from the fifteenth through the eighteenth century.

stern
(STERN)
The back end of a ship or boat; also, strict or harsh.

truce
(TROOS)
An agreement to suspend fighting.

wampum
(WOM-pum)
Beads made from polished shells and often strung on strings; used in trade for other goods.

Index